ABCNYC
A book about SEEING New York City

by JOANNE DUGAN

Design by PAMELA HOVLAND

(Inspiration from HUGO AND HENRY)

ABRAMS BOOKS FOR YOUNG READERS, NEW YORK

A is for **ATLAS**. He cannot wave to you because he is carrying the world on his shoulders.

B is for **BAGEL**. Some say they are better with butter.

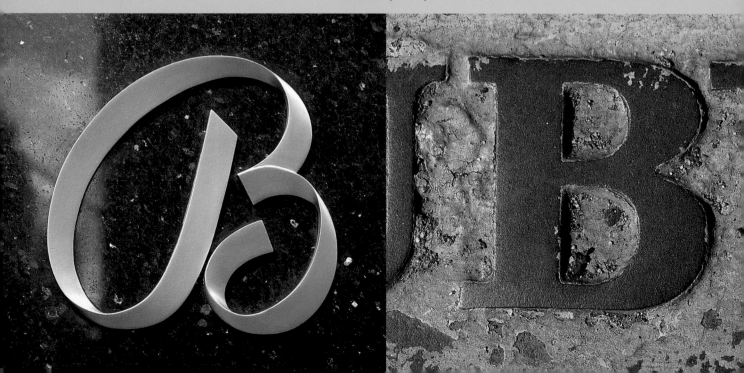

C is for **CHRYSLER BUILDING**. It sparkles silver on a sunny day.

D is for **DOG**. Meet Snoop, Biggie, Kira, Axel, Lucy, Lulu, Cookie, Ms. Ping, and Timothy.

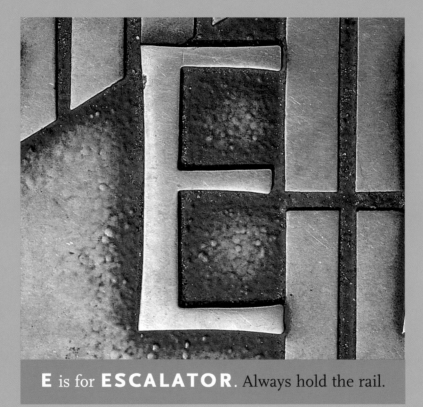

E is for **ESCALATOR**. Always hold the rail.

F is for **FLATIRON BUILDING**. It is one of the flattest skyscrapers in Manhattan.

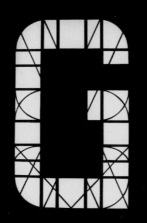

G is for **GRAND CENTRAL**.

And it is very grand indeed.

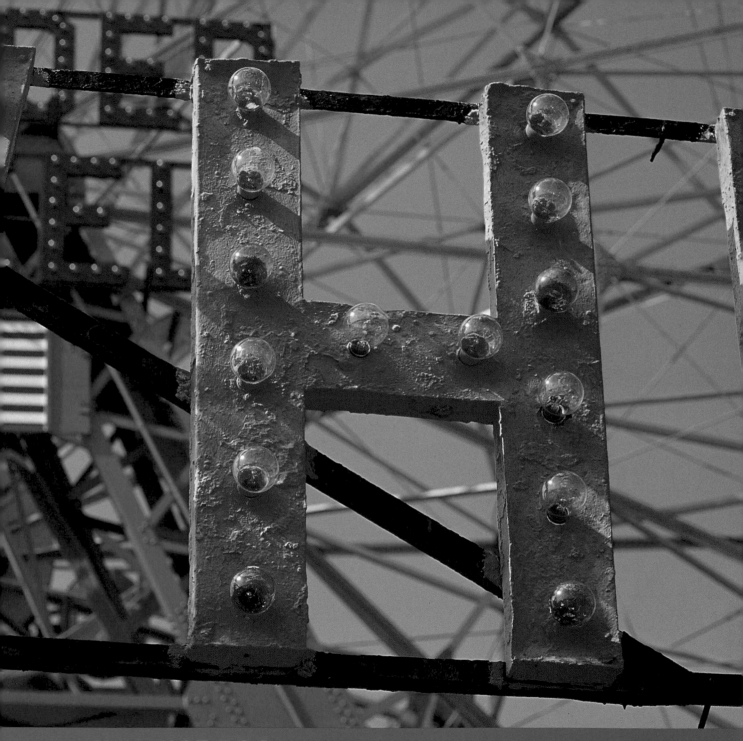

H is for **HOT DOG**. Ketchup, mustard, relish, onions, cheese, or sauerkraut?

I is for **ICE SKATE**.

Glide in winter or summer.

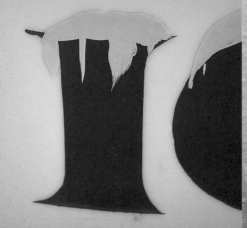

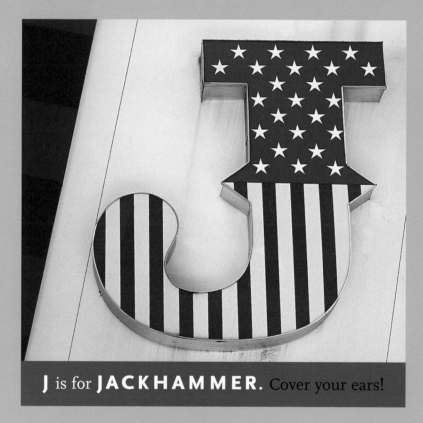

J is for **JACKHAMMER.** Cover your ears!

K is for **KEYS.** A building superintendent carries the keys to many doors.

L is for **LITTLE RED LIGHTHOUSE.** It lives under the George Washington Bridge.

M is for **MANHOLE COVER**. There are more than 500,000 to jump on.

N is for **NEWSSTAND**.

You can buy more than news.

O is for **OBELISK**. This Central Park monument is much older than your grandmother.

P is for **PENGUIN**. Watch them at the zoo.

Q is for **QUEENSBOROUGH**.

Q

Bridge, that is.

R is for **RICE**. Can you eat it with chopsticks?

S is for **SUBWAY**. Take a train from A to Z.

T is for **TAXI**. Stop one by holding your hand up in the air.

U is for **UNISPHERE**. Take the subway to Queens to see the world's largest globe.

V is for **VIEW**.

There is one out every window.

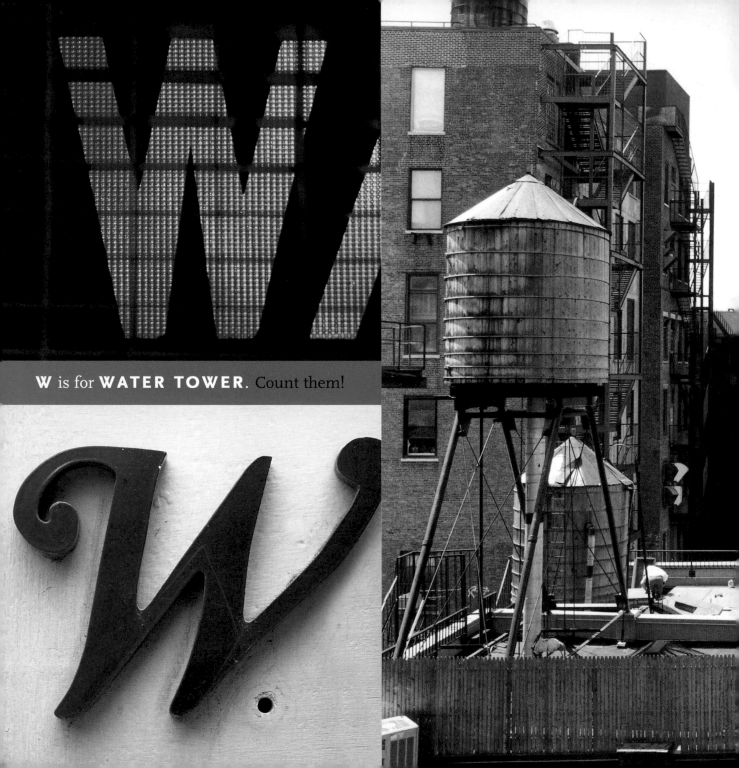

W is for **WATER TOWER**. Count them!

X is for **XYLOPHONE.** Street performers play their music all day and night.

Y is for **YARMULKE**. These small caps come in many patterns and colors.

Z is for **ZOOM**. New York City never stops!

Location, location, location

COVER
A: Newly sprayed graffiti on the Lower East Side.
B: A bicycle shop on West 14th Street.
C: The C train subway sign on 23rd Street and 8th Avenue.
N: The terrazzo entranceway at Howard Johnson's on Times Square, where fried clams are on the menu.
Y: Gordon's Novelty at Broadway and 21st Street (sadly, now closed).
C: Handpainted letters at a deli on 14th Street.

ENDPAPERS
Inside front: A view from a 12th floor rooftop on Union Square West looking north; inside back: A crowd on 45th Street and Broadway in Times Square.

ALPHABET SPREADS
A: Howard Johnson's on Times Square; Atlas stands proud at Rockefeller Center on East 50th Street at Fifth Avenue. Image of Atlas used with permission of RCPI Landmark Properties, LLC.
B: A "B" scratched into a brick storefront on East 18th Street; a garage door on West 49th Street; Bloomingdale's on 59th Street and Lexington Avenue; sidewalk grate on 14th Street and Fifth Avenue; bagels bought while still warm at H&H.
C: Gordon's Novelty at Broadway and 21st Street; sunny day view of the Chrysler Building from the northeast corner of 45th Street and Second Avenue.
D: Broadway theater ad in Times Square; Snoop was photographed on the cobblestones on Gansevoort Street; Biggie in Tompkins Square Park; Kira at the annual Dachshund Spring Fiesta in Washington Square Park; Axel at home; Lucy on Lexington Avenue and 36th Street with Justine; Lulu in Washington Square Park; Cookie in his mom's jacket in Union Square Park; Ms. Ping at the dog run in Tompkins Square Park; and Timothy in Washington Square Park.
E: Fifth Avenue Art Deco sidewalk signage; Thomas was photographed riding up on the escalator in the Winter Garden at the World Financial Center.
F: Signage at the "Shoot the Freak" attraction at Coney Island; a parking lot sign on 45th Street between Ninth and Tenth Avenues; a refreshment stand at Coney Island; the Film Center Cafe on Ninth Avenue. The Flatiron Building was shot on the little cement island on 23rd Street and Fifth Avenue, looking south.
G: Downtown 4 train during rush hour; Grand Central Terminal main concourse looking east on a sunny day.
H: The Wonder Wheel at Coney Island; long dogs, short dogs, dogs with toppings, and dogs without were shot at Nathan's at Coney Island; the Central Park Boatpond; and Staten Island. Special thanks to Thomas, Henry, and Aniya.
I: Two "icy Is" were shot at Coney Island, the city's largest resource for signs that have letters with ice on them. Another one was from an ice store on far West 49th Street. The skating twins, Fifi and Roro, were shot at the Chelsea Piers ice skating rink.
J: The patriotic "J" was found at 170th Street and Townsend off the Grand Concourse in the Bronx; the jackhammer man was making a racket on lower Broadway in Manhattan.
K: Graffiti in a parking lot on East 17th Street between Broadway and Fifth Avenue, a great spot to see the latest writing styles. The keys are from John Vella, the super of a building on Union Square West that is more than one hundred years old. John took over the job from his father, Manny, who started there in the first week of February in 1962.
L: A diner on West 23rd Street; Coney Island skee ball booth; Coney Island food stand; tile signage was created by Jim Power, the "Mosaic Man" of the East Village. The Little Red Lighthouse sits under the George Washington Bridge, on 181st Street and the Hudson River.
M: Letterform on the floor of an elevator on East 17th Street; manholes were found in the East Village, the meatpacking district, Brooklyn Heights, and Cobble Hill.
N: A *New York Times* newspaper dispenser on Fifth Avenue. Noah and Amos were photographed at a newsstand in Grand Central Station.
O: "O" in the Central Park Zoo sign; Obelisk in Central Park behind the Metropolitan Museum of Art.
P: Signage at P.S.1 art museum in Queens. Visit these Gentoo and Chipstrap penguins in the Children's Zoo in Central Park.
Q: Sign from the Q subway train; Queensborough Bridge as seen from 58th Street and the East River.
R: Ratner's on Delancey Street. Emily was photographed in the Mee Noodle Shop on Second Avenue.
S: Sign on the Spring Street 6 train; subway was at the Yankee Stadium stop in the Bronx. You can take the A, B, C, D, E, F, G, H, J, M, N, Q, R, S, V, W and Z trains here in NYC . . . look for the letters!
T: KenTile Floors sign in Gowanus, Brooklyn, visible from the Brooklyn Queens Expressway; Lia hailing a taxi on 42nd Street; other cabs shot around town.
U: The letter "U" at the Union Square W Hotel; Unisphere at Flushing Meadows Park in Queens.
V: "V" on a hardware store sign on West 23rd Street; "V" on Surf Avenue at Coney Island; "V" on a garbage bin on Park Avenue; view from a bus leaving the Lincoln Tunnel.
W: "Walk/Don't Walk" sign; fancy storefront on 72nd Street; water tower view from an 11th floor women's bathroom window on Union Square.
X: Lenox Lounge in Harlem; Roman, the xylophone player, performed for Victoria on Gansevoort Street.
Y: "Y" on an egg-cream-shop sign on 187th Street in the Bronx, near Arthur Avenue; yarmulkes shot around town.
Z: Pizza sign on Houston Street; Central Park Zoo sign. Zoom is a view moving very fast through the Lincoln Tunnel!

BACK COVER
Hugo and Joanne shopping at the Union Square Farmer's Market.

THE IDEA FOR THIS BOOK came while I was teaching the letters of the alphabet to my two-year-old son, Hugo. My family lives in the middle of Manhattan in a not particularly quiet part of town. In our neighborhood there are no shopping malls or front yards. Most New Yorkers don't own SUVs, doghouses, tool sheds, or lobster pots. Our stuff is the stuff of small spaces and urban life.

One day Hugo and I began to read through the many ABC books given to us by well wishers after he was born. There were the usual suspects: B for Bunny, C for Cow. I realized that it was going to be a while before he encountered any of these things in person. The books we owned didn't take into account that city kids have a different visual vocabulary.

I walked down the street with Hugo and began to notice the unique New York City alphabet that was visible everywhere we looked: C was for Chrysler Building, W was for Water tower, M was for Manhole cover. We began to search out letters on everything from the signs on the subway to the graffiti on buildings. Hugo started to learn the alphabet. I took lots of pictures. And the book was born.

ABC NYC is a tribute to our great city, as seen through the eyes of its children. And as for Hugo and the alphabet, my New Yorker sensibility rests easy knowing he learned first that B is for Bagel, rather than Bunny.

JOANNE DUGAN

A very special thank you to Hugo and Ludovic Moulin, Henry Lawrence Hovland, and Steven Lawrence.

Thank you to Howard Reeves, Tamar Brazis, Becky Terhune, Eric Himmel, Lizzie Himmel, Annette Dugan, and Brett Vadset; the Dugan family; Anne Alexander, Thomas, Justine, Matthew, and Philip Enny; Emily D'Angelica and Nancy Bodurtha; Nina Kramer, Lia, and Michael Mojica; Andrew and Daisy Tom; Ann Lemon, Amos and Dane Burkhart; Allyson, Bert, and Robert Spencer; Noah and Sung Mi Kimura; Victoria and Mary Pannell; Aniya Smith; Fifi, Roro, Cot, Sophie van Wingerden, and J.J. Gass.

Thanks to the dog owners and their dogs: Jacqueline Thaw and Snoop, Ruby Struik and Cookie, Cara Brophy and Lulu, Mark Jensen and Biggie, Victoria Krasnakevich and Ms. Ping, Jay Lyons, Darius Nichols and Lucy, Maria Park and Kira, Kelly Gunn and Timothy, and finally, Axel.

Additional thanks to Jennifer Bezjak, Christine Lebeck, Eric Wolf, Paula Zanger, Roman Lankios, Stacey Lieberman, Bruce and Sarah Prince, John Vella, Andrew Berger, Christine Bauch, David Campbell, Don Wahlig, Debra Hovland, and Eva Pattis.

Library of Congress Control Number: 2001012345

Photographs and text © 2005 JOANNE DUGAN PHOTOGRAPHY, LLC
Design © 2005 PAMELA HOVLAND
Production Manager: Jonathan Lopes

Printed and bound in China
10 9 8 7 6 5

HNA
harry n. abrams, inc.
a subsidiary of La Martinière Groupe
115 West 18th Street
New York, NY 10011
www.hnabooks.com